St. John Lutheran
4th grade
Zeckzer

D0093940

The Jewel Thief's Regret

·····································

Zig Ziglar with Annie Regan

Tyndale House Publishers, Inc.   Wheaton, Illinois

Illustrations by Mary Beth Schwark
First printing, September 1987
Library of Congress Catalog Card Number 86-72351
ISBN 0-8423-1882-8
Copyright 1987 by Zig Ziglar
All rights reserved
Printed in the United States of America

The Victory

Shep Holden strode down the hallway, full of confidence. It had been a good day. Stopping in front of his locker, he closed his eyes. Mr. Michael's voice still echoed in his memory:

"As principal of Lincoln Middle School, I'm honored to present your new student body president. I give you Arthur Holden, affectionately known to us as 'Shep.' I believe Shep has a few words."

The auditorium had rung with applause as Shep walked to the podium, his sister, Mandy, flashing the victory sign from the front row. "Thank you very much. . . ." Shep smiled to himself now as he remembered his own words.

"It was a tough campaign. I want to thank my

5

opponent, Jimmy Hamilton, for keeping me on my toes. It was an exciting race."

He had looked straight at Jimmy, addressing him personally. "Jimmy, it was close. I wish you and your running mates the best."

Jimmy had wanted badly to be president. *Maybe too much,* Shep thought as he twirled the combination on his lock. *I think he wanted it more to make himself look good than to make the school better. But that's just my opinion, and anyway, the campaign's over.*

There had been "dirty tricks," like on the night of Open House. Shep and Paul, his campaign manager, had spent the afternoon plastering the school with election posters. Shep's smiling face framed in gold above green lettering had proclaimed "Shep for Progress" in twenty-five locations before they left the campus for dinner.

"Pretty impressive," Paul had told Shep as they returned for Open House. Instead, it turned out pretty dumb.

Someone had taken a black marker and had changed every poster into a picture of Mickey Mouse, or rather Sheppy Mouse. The green lettering had been blackened out, while new lettering had been inked in reading, "Sheppy for Mouse-keteer."

No one had seen the vandals, but Shep knew Jimmy was behind the "joke." There had been other irritations such as missing notes before an important speech and silly proposals for the school posted in his name. But Shep hadn't been able to link Jimmy to any of them.

Well, forgive and forget, he thought now as he opened his locker. A gush of blue slime made forgetting almost impossible.

Someone had filled a pail with a stinky blue substance and had positioned it inside his locker so that it would pour out when he opened the door.

"Jimmy!" Shep muttered the name under his breath. "You'll pay for this." He looked down at his ruined pants and shoes, the blue stuff oozing onto the floor. "I should make you clean up this mess on your hands and knees."

But as usual, Shep had no proof. And as usual, he had to take care of the mess himself.

"I could handle it better if Jimmy would fight out in the open," he later told Paul as they walked home. "Talk about a coward!"

Paul shook his head. "I can't believe he wants to

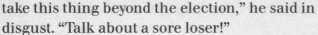

take this thing beyond the election," he said in disgust. "Talk about a sore loser!"

"I'm going to get him back," Shep said quietly. "I took it all during the campaign. I resisted the urge to give it to him then. I didn't want to be guilty of sabotage. But this is different. This is personal."

Instead of doing his homework that evening, Shep spent the time plotting his revenge. It would have to be good. He'd take his time. He wanted to pay Jimmy back once and for all, to get even so skillfully that Jimmy would transfer to another school and change his name.

I've waited this long, Shep thought. *I can wait until I find the perfect revenge. No*

Mickey Mouse stuff for me, in spite of what Jimmy thinks. When I let him have it, he'll know he's been had by an expert.

Most of what he planned that evening was too awful to be real. By the time he drifted off to sleep, Shep had fantasized everything from making Jimmy walk a plank into the ocean to stranding him on a desert island with only coconuts for food.

Jimmy haunted him throughout the night, disturbing his sleep so that Shep woke looking as if he'd slept minutes instead of hours.

"Are you sick?" his mother asked at breakfast. "Stomachache? Sore throat? Sniffles? Fever?" She felt his head. "No. Chest pain? Dizziness?" Mrs. Holden ran through the list of ordinary symptoms.

"I'm fine, Mom. Please!" Shep straightened in his chair and showed some enthusiasm for his breakfast. "I'm fine. See?" He speared a piece of sausage. "I just slept rotten. I think it was too stuffy in my room or something."

"It's all the responsibility of being president," Mandy said. "He has to make a speech this morning. It's the first student council meeting."

The sausage slipped off Shep's fork before it reached his mouth. "It's the what?" he asked.

"The first student council meeting," Mandy

repeated. "You're supposed to make a speech. Remember?"

Shep slumped back in his seat. "I remember *now*," he groaned. "But why didn't I remember last night? I haven't prepared a thing."

"Don't worry. You'll think of something." Mandy tossed her head as if to say, "It's easy!"

It's easy for you, Shep thought. *You can talk about anything at a moment's notice. But I have to prepare. And besides, I wanted this to be special. I wanted to say something meaningful for the first council meeting, something new.*

Shep's words at the council meeting were meaningful, but they weren't new. In his hurry to come up with a speech, he had gathered points from several campaign speeches and patched them into a five-minute presentation.

No one noticed, he assured himself as he raced to his English class. Relieved it was over, he just wanted to get on with the task of being president. *I'm going to make a difference in this school,* he told himself again.

Shep had campaigned for progress. "Lincoln Middle School needs spirit," he had told his listeners. "We can make a difference in our school, our community, and our own lives. We can be proud of ourselves. We are the future. We are the America of tomorrow."

By the time Shep arrived for his meeting with Mr. Michael that afternoon, he was in control again.

After his lukewarm speech at the student council meeting, he had taken the time to list his goals for the year. *I'll concentrate on this right now,* he had told himself as he studied the yellow sheet of paper, *and think about Jimmy over the weekend.*

"Shep!" Mr. Michael greeted him

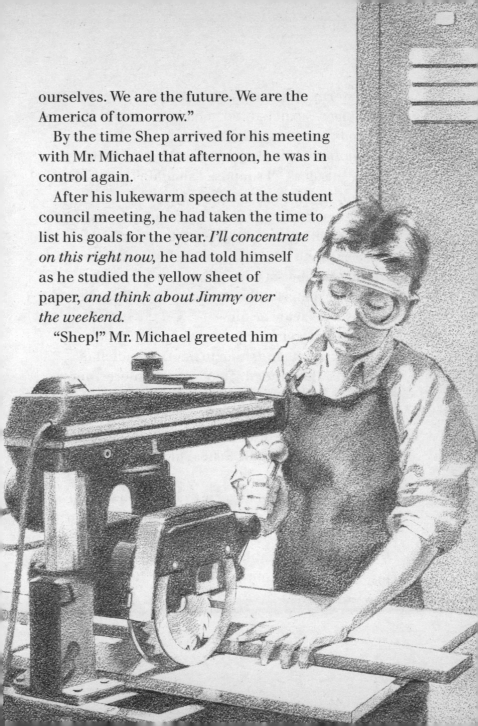

with a warm smile and a firm handshake. "I want you to know I'm delighted to have you as our student body president this year."

He motioned for Shep to sit in the tan leather chair by his desk. "I suppose I shouldn't take sides, but in my opinion, the best man won."

"Uh, thank you, sir." Shep felt his cheeks flush at the principal's praise. "I'll do my best, sir."

"I'm sure you will." Mr. Michael walked to his swivel chair and sat down. "Now tell me again about your plans for the student body." He waved a hand as if to clear the air.

"I've heard your campaign speeches, but this time I want to hear it, man to man, president to principal." He grinned. "You have an interesting point of view."

Shep beamed. "It's just that I think we should make a difference in Three Forks. I think the students of Lincoln Middle School have a lot to give our town."

He leaned forward eagerly as he warmed to his subject. "I think we should put the things we learn in school to use in real life.

"We made lamp tables and bookends in my shop class last year. My mother liked mine because I made them, but she didn't really need them. That started me thinking.

"A shop class could just as easily take on a community project for the semester. Planters for the old folks' home or repairing the benches in the park." Shep talked for several minutes, throwing out ideas on how the middle school students could use their learning to benefit the town.

Mr. Michael laughed when he was through. "I like the way you think," he said, reaching to shake Shep's hand again. "You've convinced me. One of these days, you'll be up for mayor." He stood to walk Shep to the door. "You've got an idea for everything."

Everything except for how to get even with Jimmy Hamilton, Shep thought as he walked home.

He kept Jimmy locked in a corner of his mind the rest of the week. He concentrated on his studies and his new role as student body president, avoiding Jimmy at school until Friday afternoon.

The school grounds were almost empty by the time he finished photocopying handouts in the office and walked to his locker. Jimmy was waiting for him.

"Heard things got kind of gooey for you this

week, Mouseketeer," Jimmy called, his voice taunting. "Wonder what's in your locker now?" He gave Shep's locker a big thump. "That's the way it's going to be, Hot Shot, all year long. I hear you'll never know what's coming your way."

"Is that a threat?" Shep's voice was like ice. "What goes around comes around."

"Is that a threat?" Jimmy threw back his head and howled, long and loud. "You don't scare me, Mr. Goodie Boy. You don't scare me at all." He pounded Shep's locker again and walked off.

"Just remember," he called as he rounded the corner. "You'll never know when it's coming. Never."

The Gentleman Thief

CHAPTER

2

Instead of going out with the gang for pizza that night, Shep locked himself in his room to plan his revenge. Although his ideas were more realistic this time, none of them seemed right.

It has to be practical, clever, and final, he reminded himself as he turned off the light. *Maybe it'll come to me tonight.* But the only thing that came to him in his fitful sleep was Jimmy's face. "You'll never get me. You aren't smart enough," it sneered.

That's the problem, Shep thought as he trudged up to Uncle Zig's house for work the next morning. *I'm not underhanded enough to pay Jimmy back on his own terms. But I'll learn!*

"Shep!" Uncle Zig waved from an upstairs window. "I'm glad you could make it. The lawn needs you. I'll be right down."

Shep waved back halfheartedly. *He's always so positive about things,* he thought as Uncle Zig disappeared. *I wonder what he'd do about Jimmy Hamilton.*

Uncle Zig found Shep in the toolshed behind the house, a rake in one hand and a broom in the other. "I want to shake your hand, Mr. President!" he said, booming out his enthusiasm for Shep's new title. He took the rake in his left hand and extended his right.

"I've had the honor of shaking the president's hand in Washington," he said, pumping Shep's hand, "but I'm just as proud to be shaking yours. If there's anything I can do to help, please ask me."

"Thank . . . thank you, sir." Shep stuttered uncertainly, taken aback by Uncle Zig's gusto. "Actually, there is a project." He had wanted help on something right away, but now he couldn't remember what.

"It has to do with fund-raising." They stepped out into the sunlight, and Shep searched the landscape, hoping for a clue to what his idea had been. "I have an idea. I thought you might give me your opinion. But, uh, I need a little more time."

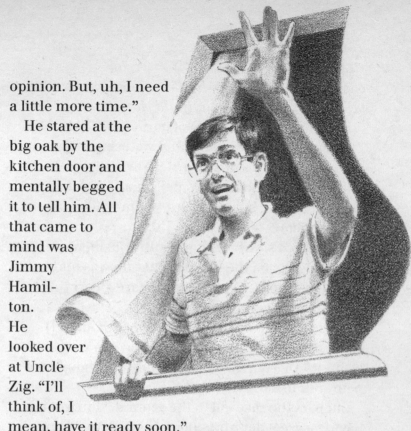

He stared at the big oak by the kitchen door and mentally begged it to tell him. All that came to mind was Jimmy Hamilton. He looked over at Uncle Zig. "I'll think of, I mean, have it ready soon."

"Anytime you want." Uncle Zig clapped him on the back. "I'll be gone next week, but I'll be home on the weekend." He handed Shep the rake, turned to walk away, and added, "Come on in the house when you need a cool drink."

"Thanks." Shep put down the broom. *It must feel good to be the number-one salesman in America,* he thought. *Right now, I'd settle for being the number-*

*one student at Lincoln Middle School. And I could
be, too, if it weren't for slimy old Hamilton.*

Shep had done all kinds of gardening for Uncle
Zig, planting and weeding and watering, but raking
autumn leaves was his favorite. Normally, their
unique colors and musty smells made him feel
glad to be alive, but today they seemed like just
another chore.

He worked slowly without enthusiasm, his mind
on Jimmy, not on the season. The sun was high
overhead when Uncle Zig reappeared, carrying
two sodas on ice.

"You didn't come in," he said. "So I thought I'd
come out. Take a break. You've been working long
enough." He studied Shep carefully. "Although not
with your usual style."

Shep let the rake fall to the ground. "I'm just not
having a great day," he said as he sank to the grass.

Uncle Zig handed him the soda and joined him
on the lawn. "Want to talk about it?" he asked.

Shep shook his head. "It's something I have to
take care of myself."

"Oh." Uncle Zig took a sip and waited.

Shep drained his glass and put it to his forehead, the cool surface pressing against the headache he felt building. "I could tell you this story, though. You're always telling us stories. Want to hear one of mine?"

"Tell away." Uncle Zig took another sip.

"Well, there was this guy, this man." Shep settled back on his hands, the glass discarded beside him. "He ran for . . . mayor of . . . of a small town," he went on, thinking quickly to disguise his story. "The man's opponent in the race didn't exactly play fair. But the man just put up with it. He was sure the 'dirty tricks' would stop when the race was over, so he didn't try to get even.

"He wanted to win because he was the best guy for the job, not because he'd made the other guy look dumb. Well, anyway, the man won and got to be mayor, but . . ."

When Shep had finished, Uncle Zig thought for a while, nodding now and then before he answered. Then he said, "I'll tell you a story for your story. You think about it while I'm gone and give me your opinion next Saturday."

Shep stretched out to listen, feeling better already.

"My story begins in the 1920s, the Roaring Twenties, when this country was prosperous and people thought war was over for good." Uncle Zig crossed his legs in a storytelling pose. "A man named Arthur Barry thought he'd take advantage of all this prosperity.

"He became a jewel thief, perhaps the most outstanding jewel thief of all time. People nicknamed him the 'Gentleman Thief' because he was a snob. He gained an international reputation for stealing only from the top of society."

Uncle Zig laughed. "In fact, it became a status symbol," he went on. "If the 'Gentleman Thief' chose you to steal from, it meant you had not only money and jewels, but position, too.

"One night, Arthur Barry was caught during a robbery and shot three times. With bullets in his body and splinters of glass in his eyes, he was suffering terrible pain, but he made a sensible statement: 'I'm never gonna do that again.'

"Surprisingly, he escaped and stayed out of jail for three years. Then, a jealous woman turned him in, and he served an eighteen-year sentence. But when he was released, he kept his word. He didn't go back to the life of a jewel thief. Instead, he settled in a small New England town and became a model citizen.

"Eventually, word leaked out that Arthur Barry,

the famous jewel thief, lived in this little town.
Reporters from all over the country came to
interview him. They asked many questions,
but none as piercing as the one asked by
a young reporter.

" 'Mr. Barry, you stole from a lot
of wealthy people during your
years as a thief,' this reporter said, 'but I'm
curious to know if you
remember the one from
whom you stole the
most.' "

Uncle Zig stopped and
Shep sat up, urging him
on. "What did he say? It
must have taken him
awhile to remember—
he'd stolen from so many."

Uncle Zig shook
his head. "No.

Mr. Barry answered right away. He said, 'That's easy. The man from whom I stole the most was Arthur Barry. I could have been a successful businessman, a baron on Wall Street, and a contributing member of society. But instead I chose the life of a thief, and I spent two-thirds of my adult life behind prison bars.' "

Uncle Zig stood and reached down for the soda glasses. "Shep, what Arthur Barry stole from others could never match what he stole from himself." He looked directly into Shep's eyes. "Your *mayor* would do well to remember the jewel thief's regret."

"What a story!" Shep said to himself as he went back to his raking. "A real socker!"

It fits Jimmy perfectly, he thought as he walked home. *Jimmy's just like Arthur Barry! He's a smart kid. He could have a lot going for him. But instead of working for himself in the campaign, he just worked against me. He tried to sabotage me, but he really only sabotaged himself because he lost the race.*

What I can't figure out, he thought as he went to bed, *is why Uncle Zig told me that story. Maybe he wants me to pass it on to Jimmy so he'll realize what he's doing and stop.*

It seemed unlikely. Shep knew Jimmy wouldn't

sit still long enough to hear the story, much less think about its meaning. He laughed at the scene that came to mind.

It would never work! he told himself, picturing the unbelievable. *I'm opening my locker and out jumps this snake. Probably not poisonous, but I can't stand snakes of any kind. I scream and run away. Jimmy's down the hall, laughing his head off. I come up to him and say, "I can't prove you put that snake in my locker, but I know you did it.*

"Now sit down and I'm going to fix your wagon. I'm going to tell you this story about a jewel thief. It's going to make you realize you're throwing your life away by being an underhanded creep. After you hear this story, you'll ask my forgiveness and change your ways."

Shep went to sleep laughing and dreamed about lecturing Jimmy on the error of his ways until he was down on his knees pleading for mercy.

The Revenge

In the days that followed, Shep dismissed Uncle Zig's story as impossible to explain to Jimmy and therefore of no help to him with his problem. *The only thing that will help me now is a clever plan to show Jimmy up for the creep he really is,* he repeated.

Shep's work on the student council slowed to a halt as he spent more and more time plotting how to get even. His talent for cartooning, often used for the school newspaper, went instead to comic book sketches predicting Jimmy's downfall. On Saturdays he sent Paul to work in his place, unable to face Uncle Zig with his conclusion.

Three weeks after his official meeting as student

body president with Mr. Michael, the principal called him back to his office.

"I'm concerned about you, son," he said after Shep was seated in the leather chair. "I pass you in the hallways, and it's as if someone's turned out the lights."

"I'm fine!" Shep sat on the edge of the chair and repeated it. "I'm fine. Really! I'm fine." But his voice seemed too loud, his smile too fixed.

"Your teachers say your grades are tumbling." Mr. Michael frowned.

"It's tougher this year than I thought it would be."

"Your teachers say you doodle. They say you draw cartoons during class."

"I'm practicing. I might be a cartoonist someday."

"But today you are student body president." Mr. Michael went to the window. "And a month ago, you were full of enthusiasm. Now I hear the council's going nowhere. Nothing's happening."

He looked out at the students rushing from class to class, then back at Shep. "Arthur, what's happening? What's troubling you?"

"Nothing," Shep protested again, but it rang false the moment he spoke. "Well, something. But I have to solve it myself. It's a . . . it's a personal thing."

Mr. Michael tapped on the desk for a moment

and then said, "Shep, for your own good and the good of Lincoln Middle School, I feel I should have a talk with your parents."

"Please don't, sir!" Shep stood up nervously. "They're already worried about me. Give me another week. If I haven't solved it by then . . ." His voice trailed off. He didn't know what. He just knew he was desperate to strike a bargain.

"All right," Mr. Michael agreed uncertainly. "But no more doodling in class. Promise?"

"Promise," Shep said heartily.

"And a week from now, I expect to see the old Shep Holden walking the halls."

What am I going to do now? Shep asked himself as he walked home alone after school. *What's going to change in a week? I've thought and thought until my brain's ready to pop.*

I can't come up with anything. Everything I've thought of only increases the conflict and makes me look like another Jimmy Hamilton.

Not ready to face Mandy or his mother at home, he took a detour on Blossom Street and walked aimlessly down the sidewalk, the last traces of autumn unnoticed about him. He turned left off Blossom Street and right several blocks later, then left again.

"Hi!" A small voice caught his ear from a side yard. "You're the present of the world, aren't you?"

Shep laughed and turned to see a tiny blonde girl holding onto a big brown bear. "I'm the *president* of the middle school, not of the world," he said kindly. "How did you know?"

"I know all stuff." The little girl gave the teddy a squeeze.

"Yeah." Shep laughed again and started to walk on when he realized he was standing in front of the Hamilton's house. "You're Jimmy's sister, aren't

you? You're Ivy. You saw my poster. That's how you know who I am!"

Ivy backed away. "Don't tell him," she whispered, bringing a finger to her lips. "He don't know."

"Know what?" Shep whispered, too.

"That I got his bear."

"That's Jimmy's bear?" Shep pointed at the worn-looking animal, its fur bald and its ears chewed.

Ivy nodded. "He can't sleep if he don't got it. Won't let nobody touches it." Her eyes were wide at her secret. "And he chew on the ears!"

"I gotta go now, Ivy." Shep checked his emotions to keep from giving a victory whoop. "Don't worry. I won't tell Jimmy you borrowed his bear. But you'd better put it back now. We wouldn't want anything to happen to that bear."

The cares of a thousand lifetimes seemed to roll off Shep's shoulders as he raced home. By the time he reached his front porch, the perfect revenge was complete. It was practical, clever, and final. And oh, so easy!

I'll just borrow Paul's camera, the one that takes night shots without a flash. I'll snap a roll of Jimmy in bed with his teddy. Then the next day, I'll kidnap the bear (*Ivy will help me*) *and hold it for ransom until he promises never to bother me again. The pictures will be security. I'll give him copies to make sure he keeps his word.*

It was perfect. Ivy said Jimmy couldn't sleep without the bear. *A guy can't play football if he can't sleep,* Shep told himself. *And a football player can't let everybody know he chews a teddy bear's ears at night.*

Jimmy Hamilton will have to find somebody else to mess with, he promised himself.

That evening Shep was himself again, laughing and joking with his family, calling his friends on the phone, and making plans for the next day. That night he slept better than he had in weeks. It all seemed so simple — the perfect way to end the feud with Jimmy.

On the way home from school the next day, he took a detour leading past the Hamilton house, hoping to find Ivy and coax more information out of her. A block away, he heard scuffling sounds in a vacant lot to his right and noticed a patch of bushes moving.

Shep stopped and listened. At first everything was quiet, but he waited, his head cocked to one

side, certain something was happening in the lot. In a moment, he heard scuffling again, followed by low voices.

Kids, he thought with a smile, *playing war or cowboys and Indians.* Impulsively, he walked to the bushes and stuck his head through. But instead of six-year-olds at play, he saw three large boys grouped around a smaller one. The smaller boy's arms were pinned, his mouth stuffed with a red cloth.

"Jimmy!" With a shock, Shep recognized the boy and called out his name, not considering the consequences.

"Who's that?" one of the boys growled, and the group turned to glare at Shep.

"That's nobody," the tallest boy said, his voice low and menacing.

Shep stared at Jimmy, unable to move. Jimmy's eyes, wide with panic, looked at him above a rough hand that had been thrust over his mouth. Jimmy's shirt was torn, and Shep made out a bruise on his left temple.

"Just walk away, kid, 'cause you didn't see any-thing," the tallest boy said. "You didn't see any-thing, did you?"

Shep simply stood there as if in a dream. *I could*

walk away, he thought, *and pretend I didn't see anything. Jimmy's finally getting what he deserves. This could be my revenge. I don't have to lift a finger; just turn around and walk away.*

He backed away a bit, and the boys laughed. "Yeah, he didn't see anything," one of them said.

But it's three against one, Shep's thoughts continued. *And they're so much bigger than he is. And they look so mean. Jimmy's done a hundred things to bug people, but none of them has been truly cruel.*

"Mr. Hennessey the cop lives across the street." Shep heard his own voice, loud and controlled as if it were coming from someone else. "If I scream right now, he'll hear me and come running.

"Go on right now and leave my friend alone," he commanded, though his heart, beating like a caged bird's, told him Mr. Hennessey might not even be home.

The three boys were off before Shep finished speaking. Mr. Hennessey's name was all they had needed to hear. Jimmy stood there alone, bits of grass in his hair, another bruise on his chin. "Mmmmruffrunn," he mumbled, pulling the cloth from his mouth. "You called me 'your friend'?"

The two boys looked at each other in disbelief. Then Shep laughed. "Well, I guess you are," he said

. . . .

with a shrug. "Come on out of there before those guys decide to come back."

They walked the block in silence. Then Shep asked, "What did you do to make them so mad, anyway?"

Jimmy felt his chin. "Oh, you know. The usual. Why'd you help me?"

"I'm not sure," Shep said slowly. "I think it had something to do with the mayor."

"The mayor? Was he around, too?"

"No, not our mayor. Just a mayor in a story I made up the other day."

Uncle Zig's last words came back to him. "Your *mayor* would do well to remember the jewel thief's regret." *He told that story for me,* Shep thought, *not for Jimmy,*

. . . .

although it fits him perfectly, too.

*I've been so busy planning revenge, I've been
robbing myself of my own life. And if I'd walked
away from the fight, or even blackmailed Jimmy
with his teddy bear, I would have stolen from myself
something priceless—my own sense of what's right.*

Shep turned to look at Jimmy. He was staring at
him as if Shep were an alien from Mars. "I think
you should stop doing rotten things to people," he
said frankly.

"Yeah, sure. Of course," Jimmy muttered. "I
won't do anything anymore to *you*. Don't worry."

"No, I mean you shouldn't do stuff anymore to
anybody." Shep stopped and pointed to the curb.
"Sit down. I'm going to tell you a story. . . ."

That Saturday, Shep whistled on his way up the
hill. The sky seemed brighter than he could ever
remember it, and the air was so fresh he thought
someone should bottle it and sell it in Los Angeles.

Uncle Zig greeted him from the front lawn.
"Good to see you, Shep," he called. "I was wonder-
ing when you'd be back."

Shep waited until they were standing beside
each other. Then he said, "I passed your story along
to the *mayor,* and it took him a long time to figure it
out. He's sort of the stubborn type."

"I take it he finally came up with the right answer." Uncle Zig adjusted his glasses, a twinkle in his eye.

Shep nodded. "He said to tell you he understands the jewel thief's regret, and he isn't going to make the same mistake."

"And his opponent? Is he still playing 'dirty tricks'?" Uncle Zig handed him a shovel. "I have some digging in the back," he explained, leading the way.

"His opponent retired," Shep said with a laugh. "He decided he didn't want the jewel thief's regret either."

THE END
· · · · · · · · ·